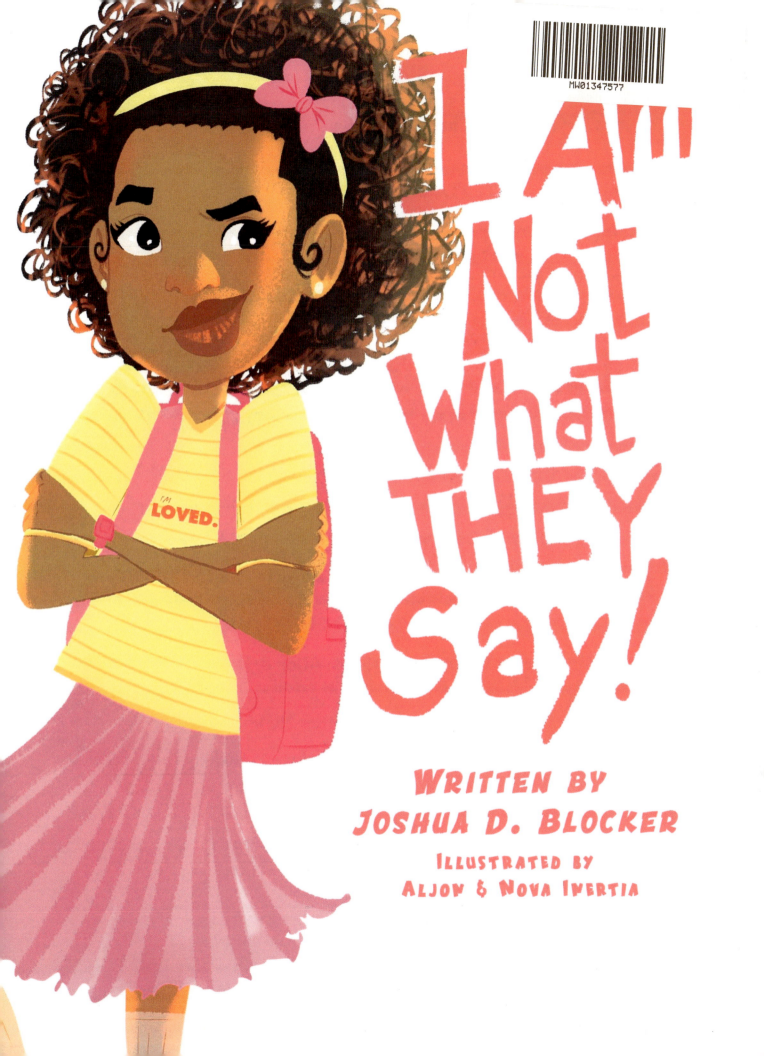

Copyright © by JuJo Publishing Co. / Joshua D. Blocker.

All rights reserved. Published in the United States by JuJo Publishing Co., a division of DAWAY ENTERTAINMENT LLC. No part of this publication may be reproduced, distributed, or transmitted in any form or by any means, including photocopying, recording, or other electronic or mechanical methods, without the prior written permission of the publisher, except in the case of brief quotations embodied in critical reviews and certain other noncommercial uses permitted by copyright law. For permission requests, write to the publisher, addressed "Attention: Permissions Coordinator," at the address below.

Boy Edition
ISBN: 978-1-7375247-0-0 (Paperback) — ISBN: 978-1-7375247-2-4 (e-book)

ISBN: 978-1-7375247-4-8 (Hardback)

Girl Edition
ISBN: 978-1-7375247-1-7 (Paperback) — ISBN: 978-1-7375247-3-1 (e-book)

ISBN: 978-1-7375247-5-5 (Hardback)

Library of Congress Control Number: 2021913257

Any references to historical events, real people, or real places are used fictitiously. Names, characters, and places are products of the author's imagination.

Cover Design/Illustrations: Aljon & Nova Inertia
Author: Joshua Blocker

First printing edition 2021.

DAWAY ENTERTAINMENT dba JuJo Publishing Co.

The Colony, TX 75056
www.dawayent.com
Email: dawayentmt@gmail.com

It's a new day, and I'm feeling light.
The sun is shining so big and so bright!
Before heading too far I drop to my knees,
I have to thank God for His brand new mercies.

To the bathroom I go for my morning routine.
As I look in the mirror, greatness stares back at me.

I jump into my clothes and land in my shoes,
while from downstairs in the kitchen
my mom shouts great news.

"Breakfast is Ready!" I take to the stairs
as cheer fills my face from all the smells!

"Mmm!" I see my favorite treats go into my lunch bag.
Mom's dressed so pretty & Dad's just so swell.

"I LOVE YOU!" they both say as I finish my plate.
"Oops we have to run before we're all late."

Before heading to work they drop me off at school.
I love my life, my parents are so cool.

Good morning to my teachers, I can't wait to learn.
A wealth of knowledge from them, I'm sure to earn.

My teacher scanned the room for helpers,
but from my peers she received none.
So I raised my hand to volunteer
because there was much work to be done.

From behind I hear their voices
saying so many things that were mean.
In awkwardness, I sat as they mocked and as they teased.
I hoped someone would rescue me and prayed the bell would ring.

Finally, after my plea!
The bell rang once and then twice,
these children are not very nice!

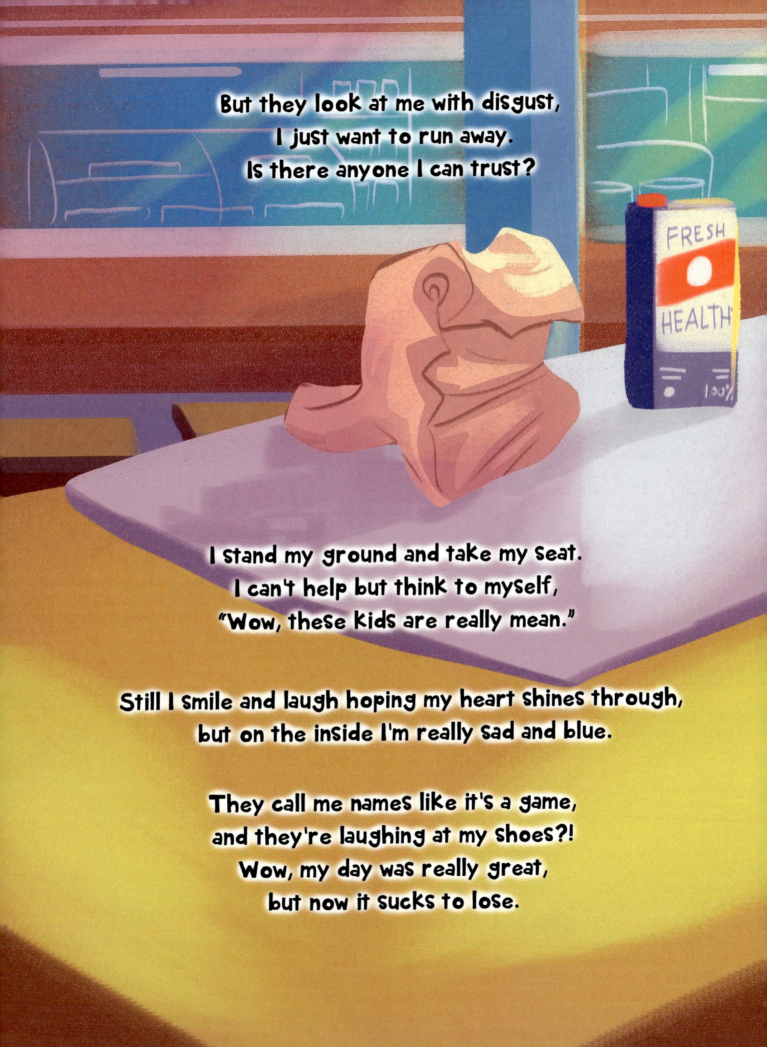

But they look at me with disgust,
I just want to run away.
Is there anyone I can trust?

I stand my ground and take my seat.
I can't help but think to myself,
"Wow, these kids are really mean."

Still I smile and laugh hoping my heart shines through,
but on the inside I'm really sad and blue.

They call me names like it's a game,
and they're laughing at my shoes?!
Wow, my day was really great,
but now it sucks to lose.

From here on out, it won't happen again.
I'll be just like them. Let the games begin!

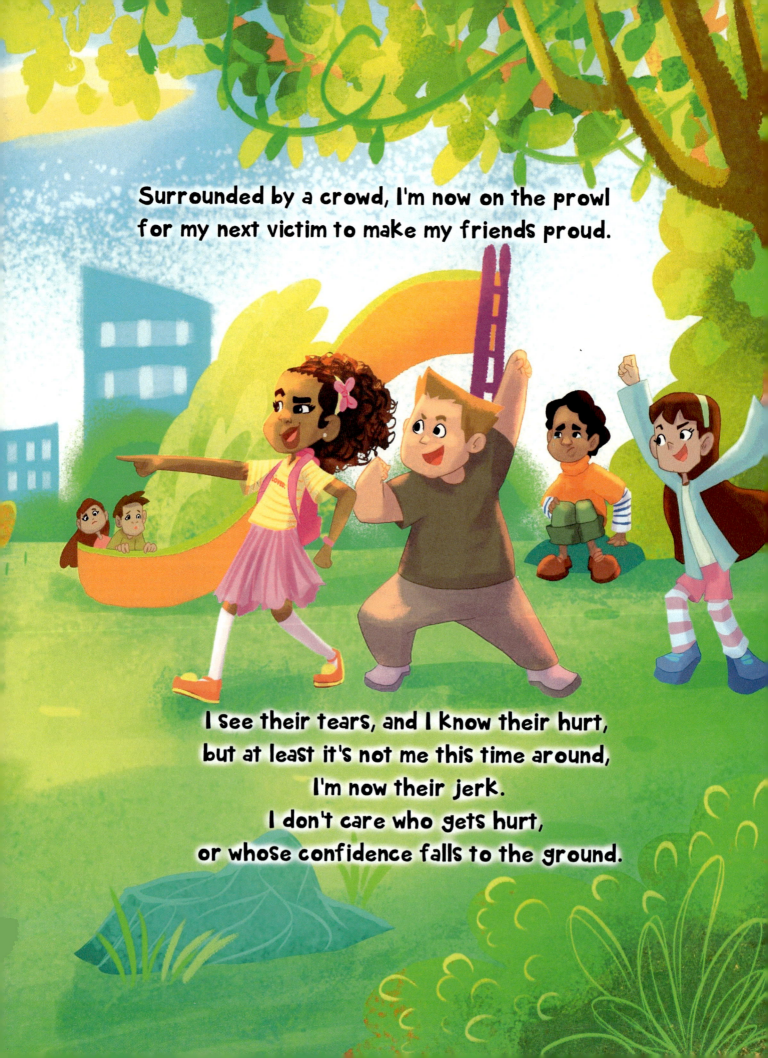

Surrounded by a crowd, I'm now on the prowl
for my next victim to make my friends proud.

I see their tears, and I know their hurt,
but at least it's not me this time around,
I'm now their jerk.
I don't care who gets hurt,
or whose confidence falls to the ground.

Surrounded by a crowd, I'm now on the prowl for my next victim to make my friends proud.

I see their tears, and I know their hurt,
but at least it's not me this time around,
I'm now their jerk.
I don't care who gets hurt,
or whose confidence falls to the ground.

The day is now over and that was kind-a-fun,
but I feel empty inside from the deeds done.

My Mom and my Dad, they're still really cool
Hey daughter hey,
what did you learn at school today?

To be mean, and deny myself, it got me accepted,
but I could never tell them that, they'd surely reject it.

So, I lie, as I smile and croon.
And once I get home, I rush to my room.
Only to find that behind the door,
There would only be gloom.

I toss and turn all through the night,
what I did just doesn't feel right.

I rush back to my room hoping to find where I left me,
but the me I had yesterday I could no longer see.
Scared out of my mind, I screamed through the pad.
As first responder and command, here comes my dad.

"I've lost who I am, but please don't be mad.
Help me find me again so I can be glad."
I told him what I'd done, yet he still called my name with love.

"YOU ARE NOT WHAT THEY SAY! YOU ARE WHO YOU ARE!
Finding YOU daughter is easy, she's not very far.

Make a decision to change your way.
It's really as simple as changing what you say."

"I Am Greatness!
I Am Success!
I Am Respectful,
so not Regretful!
I Am a Queen,
no need to be mean!

I Am Clear!
There's no need for fear!
I Am Strong!
I Am big enough to admit when I'm wrong!
I Am peace in the middle of the storm!
They could never bring me harm!
I Am LOVED,
that can never be snubbed!
I Am VALUABLE,
to be anything less is Intolerable!
I walk worthy of my call,
even after I fall."

Coming Soon
More of the Evan and Makayla Series

Grab the Boy's Edition

Also available at:
DawayEnt.com/NotWhatTheySay

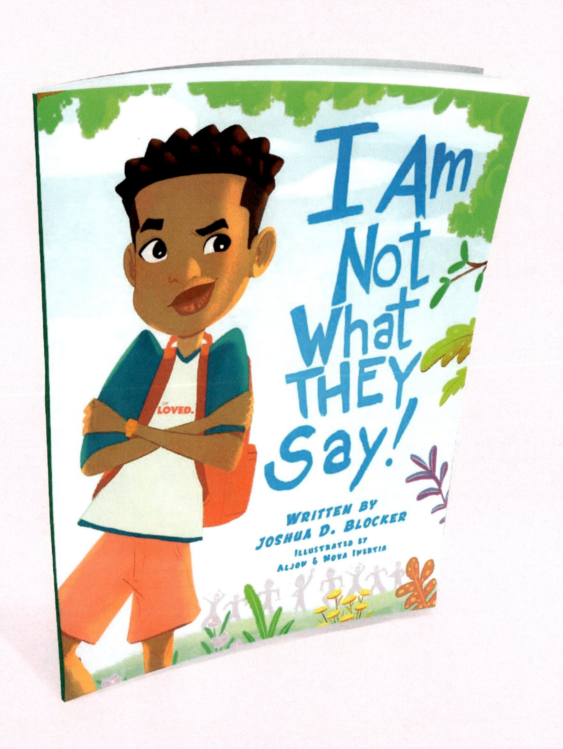

Dedication

To this pure-hearted child who chose to see only the good in people.
A child whose smile softened hearts and brightened rooms.
A child who wanted the best for everyone around him.
A child who didn't understand why being himself
caused so much criticism & ridicule.
A child who experienced many bad days but never let them change his heart.
A child who too was different and was pressured to conform
so that others would be comfortable around him.
A child who lost his way a lot of times but always found his way back.
May you always remain YOU and never reduce yourself
to becoming a you that THEY want you to be.

I dedicate this book to the boy within...
I see you, and I live to make you feel the safety you didn't feel you had.
I hope this makes you feel loved, seen, heard, and valued.

This is for children like me, different, often misunderstood, gifted,
but alone... May this always warm your heart and provide you the
reassurance you need, even when you grow up!
You are special, and I hope you know that every single day!
I LOVE YOU!

~ Josh

Acknowledgments

First, I want to thank Aljon Inertia!!! You have been an ultimate blessing and encouragement to me throughout this entire process!!
I don't even know how we got connected, but I'm so glad we did.
This idea of a book would not have happened without you!!
This was my first story for children and you BELIEVED in me!!
From our first conversation til' now, you have inspired
me to pursue this venture.
THANK YOU SO MUCH!! YOU ARE SO AMAZING

I also want to thank Teresa Velardi. Thank you for answering my questions
and helping me throughout this process.
I'm new to children's books and you have been doing this for a while.
Thank you for lending your expertise. I appreciate your kindness!!

Kevin Simpson - Thank you for being the first teacher to let me speak
to your students, to see their little eyes be lit with inspiration.
Thank you for that moment!! It pushed me to proceed.

To my Unofficial "OG" Children!! Kaitlyn, Kavon, Aaron, Jaiden(Jai),
James (Junee), Dillan..
I might be missing some but you all were my first babies..
I babysat you all and I pray that your lives are positively
influenced and impacted by my presence.
This is for all of you!! YOU CAN DO ANYTHING!!
Thanks for being my teacher, even while I was teaching you.
I LOVE YOU ALL SO MUCH!!

To my new babies, my God-Children (Saiyan & McKinley "Schmackums"),
and the brand new babies and children who love me
(ESPECIALLY, My Schnugga - Milan Robinson).
I LOVE YOU, Thank you for blessing my life!!

To the teachers, parents, coaches, etc that have purchased in bulk..
THANK YOU!!! My heart is to make life easier and better
for the children of today and tomorrow..
THANK YOU!!

Last but not least, to "The Boy Within" thanks for never giving up!!!
See what we did?!? I'm so proud of you and I want to tell you,
what you went through as a child, the things
you felt and experienced; they were NOT in vain. LOOK AT THIS!!!

About the Author

Joshua Blocker, native of Dallas, TX, is an award-winning actor, author, and all around entertainer. He has accomplished many things and has shared stages with some of the greatest talent to date.
He earned his BFA from Texas State University as a Theatre Arts major focusing on performance and production with an acting emphasis.
Since age 9, Joshua has had a heart for impacting the lives of others by way of representation.
Never chasing fame, Joshua chooses to be transparent through the power of story-telling in an effort to CHANGE LIVES.
Children are precious to Joshua; he started babysitting at age 12, and to date, children just love him!
They feel safe, seen, special, and heard with him.
It is his goal that this book, as the introduction to his children's book series, makes every child feel that same touch and power.
Joshua is dedicated to changing lives through the power of creative arts and is turning over every stone to do so.

About the Illustrators

Team Inertia – Aljon and Nova

"Team Inertia" comprises a young couple inspired to create
illustrations for children's storybooks.
Aljon specializes in creating beautiful, one-of-a-kind
illustrations for children's books. His goal and purpose in life are
to bring his passion for illustration to children's stories that
speak to good morals and values while providing
lessons for today's youth.
Aljon's colorful illustrations bring engagement to the
author's content, so the story comes alive on the book's pages.
His creative illustrations are published in children's books worldwide.

Nova was invited to team up with Aljon doing freelance projects.
She began with basic coloring, then fell in love with the creative process.
At 25, with a new career as an artist, Nova didn't realize that
her art skills are way beyond what she ever imagined.
She's found her purpose in the art industry.

I Am...

```
Q I Q P T P W Z B W L Y D U W V S Z W U V X I N
L U F T H G U O H T L T L M J P P C O L R V O B
Q E L B A U L A V D E L O T E C A X R U M R Y Y
G R V S J I Y M N K N B V C Y R Q L T F C K M K
G T T U Y Z J E V V D D I T I I S T H D V F F L
H C U O L B I Y A D N A N N M D M P Y N B J O G
L U N L U R C C K S L I G I L O N U P I W E P R
W U L U F G E N E R O U S E D U G I E M G G T A
A H I B I B R Y S Y N L A S F N J K K C L Y I T
D E Y A T X G E A Z O Y E W O N Z T N E L R M E
C A Z F U D N P L O U E N R C I T S I T R A I F
S L S H A L I R C I R H T T J J O Y F U L S S U
U T R Y E L Z C V O A S P E A C E F U L O S T L
C H G A B Q A X U K I B V C E P N E Y F M E I Z
C Y C P C J M Y P P A H L L L T C Z X Q Q C C W
E D E V O L A D E N E D N E B U F X Q F L E X Q
S K P P I E V I T A E R C A A D P P L S E N L R
S P L T R A M S V I S M S R D T W D A G I D K B
F A C S L U F R E W O P C T N A T R O P M I W J
U T T N E R E F F I D P P Z E F C H E E R F U L
L I V G N S X L U F P L E H P P A H W C P W D Q
M E I N T A L E N T E D O D E T P E C C A E C A
M N Y R E S P E C T F U L M D I G N I W O R G M
D T U N D E R S T A N D I N G F Z Q U E E N K N
```

Accepted	Grateful	Peaceful
Amazing	Growing	Powerful
Artistic	Happy	Queen
Beautiful	Healthy	Reliable
Caring	Helpful	Respectful
Cheerful	Important	Smart
Clear	Joyful	Special
Cool	Kind	Strong
Creative	Loved	Successful
Dependable	Loving	Talented
Different	Mindful	Thoughtful
Fabulous	Necessary	Understanding
Friendly	Optimistic	Valuable
Generous	Patient	Worthy

Made in the USA
Monee, IL
24 August 2021